CITYKIDS SPEAK ON
RELATIONSHIPS

Book design: Carol Mills, Sue Moberg
Photography by Bobbie Crosby
Additional photography by Brad Guice Photography, Laura Johnson, and Jane Feldman
Illustrations by Leah Teweles

Sources for Quotations:
And I Quote, compiled by Ashton Applewhite, William R. Evans III, Andrew Frothingham
Bartlett's Familiar Quotations (15th edition)
Black Pearls, by Eric V. Copage
Black Woman's Gumbo Ya-Ya, edited by Terri L. Jewell
The Concise Columbia Dictionary of Quotations, compiled by Robert Andrews
HarperBook of Quotations, edited by Robert I. Fitzhenry
Love, compiled and edited by John Train
Meditations for Women Who Do Too Much, by Anne Wilson Schaef
1,911 Best Things Anybody Ever Said, compiled by Robert Barn
The Quotable Quote Book, compiled by Merrit Malloy and Shauna Sorensen
20,000 Quips and Quotes, compiled by Evan Esar
21st Century Dictionary of Quotations, edited by the Princeton Language Institute

Jim Henson
P U B L I S H I N G™

Library of Congress Cataloging-in-Publication Data
CityKids speak on relationships.
p. cm. ISBN 0-679-86553-5
1. City children—United States—Psychology—Juvenile literature.
2. Interpersonal relations—United States—Juvenile literature. 3. Respect for persons—Juvenile literature.
[1. Interpersonal relations.] I. Title: City kids speak on relationships.
HT206.C575 1994 302—dc20 94-22823

Manufactured in the United States of America   10 9 8 7 6 5 4 3 2 1

J
302

CITYKIDS SPEAK ON
RELATIONSHIPS

Random House New York

Who Are CityKids?

It seems like everybody in the media these days is trying to reach teenagers. Music videos, magazines, fashion, TV programs, social service messages, even deodorant commercials—they're all aimed at us; they all try to define us. Everywhere we look, we're being told what to do, who to be, how to think. But nobody ever asks us what *we* think.

So we've written this book for and about young people just like us. We don't pretend to have all the answers. You might notice there is no all-knowing narrator or voice. Instead, you'll hear a lot of voices—through quotes, surveys, interviews, photographs, drawings, and, best of all, honest talk from CityKids.

Who are CityKids? We are a group of young people; we're Blacks, Whites, Yellows, Reds, of all different religious, educational, and economic backgrounds. If you look at the pictures in this book, you'll probably find someone who looks kind of like you. If you read our quotes and opinions, you'll hear things that you might have said. More important, we hope you'll hear things you never would have thought of—but will respect anyway.

The major reason we created this book is to spread an idea called Safe Space. What's Safe Space? It's the main concept of CityKids. Safe Space basically means respect—respect for yourself and respect for the people around you.

The CityKids Foundation has been around since 1985. Mostly we come from New York City. We also have members in Los Angeles, Minneapolis, Chicago, Liverpool—all over the country *and* the world. Because to be a CityKid, mostly you just need to think like a CityKid. You need to respect other people's opinions, trust your own ideas enough to share them, and invest in yourself and your power.

We hope you like the book. If you think we left anything out, please write to us. We're here.

Peace.

What's so BAD about being

What's your favrite thing to do when you've alone?

CITYKIDS SURVEY SAYS:

sit + think

I like to write

Play music   COOK

Walk   Read

meditate

What's the worst thing about not being in a couple?

CITYKIDS SURVEY SAYS:

No experience of love ♡

getting used to it   it's all bad

No one to snuggle with!

Loneliness

Nothing

you get no intimacy!

Interview with Cenophia, 17

interview

What's so bad about being alone?
Cenophia: Nothing at all.

Are you alone?
Cenophia: Yes, at the moment, I am alone.

How does it feel?
Cenophia: Feels cool. Not tied down,
not tied up either, but that's another story.
I'm free to do what I want to do.

Do you feel pressured to be with someone?
Cenophia: Yes, definitely. The sad thing is that
people who have no one pressure people to go
with someone else when actually people should
do what they feel. If you don't like someone,
then you shouldn't be with them.

Do you think it's a social stigma to be alone?
Cenophia: Not anymore. Since everyone,
even if they are with someone, pretends they
are alone.

ALONE?

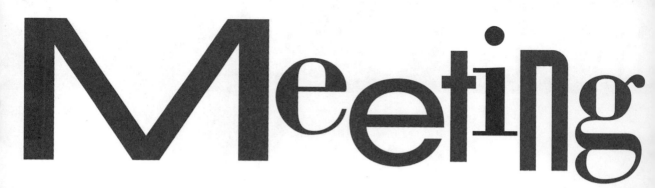

Meeting

Interview with Heather, 15, and Rob, 17

What did you think when you first saw each other?

Rob: I knew I wanted to meet her, but I didn't say anything. She has a pretty smile. She looked happy and content. It was something I knew I didn't have. Physically, she's off the charts.

Heather: He looked nice but tough. I knew I wanted to meet him, so I asked him to come hang out with my friends and me.

Rob: We hung out for a while and became friends. I knew right away I liked her, though. There was no doubt about it.

Heather: He was different because he's nicer. Most guys I had met were very single-minded from the get-go. He was slower, more respectful.

Rob: With the dating game, if there's a girl I'm attracted to, it's hard for me to talk to her. I don't know her, so it's a big step to really talk with her.

Heather: The day before I met him I told a friend of mine that I just wanted to meet someone who was nice, cute, and wouldn't mess with my head. I thought I was joking, but I swear the next day there he was.

Rob: I told her the first day I saw her that she possessed this special aura—like an angel. She's exactly the way I imagined she'd be. It frightened me and it made me feel great. Sometimes a guy can feel that a girl looks like a goddess and it makes him speechless. I still feel like that about Heather sometimes. It's scary to have a good, strong relationship. I'd never had one. I'd been hurt a lot. When you're used to something, it's scary to try something new.

Any advice for people who are looking?

Rob: Don't look for it. It happens. You just gotta relax. What you deserve will come to you. You're bound to find somebody who loves you who you can love.

Heather: Let people get to know you. Don't push people away before you've given them a chance.

Peop_le

I like this guy now and I want to tell him, but I know he doesn't like me in that way. But I can't help but like him. I think if I go up to him and tell him he'll think I'm a freak. I've got sensitive skin! Anyway, it sucks. And even if he did like me, I'd never know 'cause I'll never tell him.

Alicia, 17

My ex-girlfriend was going out with this guy for like a year. I met her and things really clicked. She broke up with him to go out with me. The whole time we were going out, though, I thought she wanted to be with him. I could never trust her because of the way the whole thing started.

Philippe, 18

I met a guy when I went to Europe. I met him at a wedding and I thought there was no other guy like him. He was nice and sweet. What made me feel so good inside was the way he would look at me—searching my face for questions he could not ask me. At the wedding, we danced together, laughed, and stared at each other from across the room. We said nothing to each other, until the end of the night. I was standing there by the doorway and I saw him standing across the room with his friends and I could feel the weight of his stare. He finally came over to me and asked me what my name was. It was a brief conversation. When we were departing, I passed him and our eyes met. That was the last time I saw him. But in my heart I know that someday we will meet to form one.

Sediga. 16

what's the
attraction?

QUICK TAKES

What do you do to make yourself more attractive?

To make myself more attractive I…

- try to have good posture and strut down the street.
- look in the mirror for a half an hour until I feel beautiful.
- wear blue things because blue makes my eyes look nice.
- exercise.
- try to be happy with myself.
- bathe regularly and shave.
- wear see-through shirts with purple bras.
- feel confident about things in general.
- pull my hair back off my neck and put on my favorite jeans.
- need a girlfriend.
- have to be in a certain mood.

People say I'm "full-figured," "fluffy," and "big-boned," so no one seems to be attracted to me—except grown men. But that is not my style. I know that I have a pretty face, but people don't usually look past my body. So I get the raw end of the deal when it comes to relationships. I'd like a nice, friendly, compassionate, relatively handsome young man who's under 21 years of age. I know they're out there, but I don't know where!

Cecilia, 17

Among those whom I like or admire, I can find no common denominator, but among those whom I love, I can: all of them make me laugh.
—W. H. Auden

If you're not feeling good about you, what you're wearing outside doesn't mean a thing.
—Leontyne Price

CAN MEN AND WOMEN

If you're friends with a guy, you start to notice

that he is so great. And then you start thinking,

well, if he is so great then why am I just friends with

him? But it doesn't always work out like that,

because the other person might not feel that way,

and if you go ahead with the relationship,

it might mess up the friendship.

—*Jennifer, 16*

BE FRIENDS?

Tanya: Ladies—

Dan: And gentlemen.

Tanya: *(annoyed)* Ladies, and I know there have to be a lot of you out there who feel disrespected like I do, when a guy you don't know comes out of nowhere with some rude come-on.

Dan: Hold up! Guys, you know that women feel flattered if you compliment them on their looks.

Tanya: What you did was not a compliment.

Dan: All I did was say that you look good.

Tanya: Ha!

Dan: What? Is it so wrong to express my attraction to such a beautiful young—

Tanya: Are you quite finished?

Dan: In case you were wondering what her problem is, this is what happened. We were in the hall at school, right? I was on my way to class when she passed by. And she did look good. So I stopped her *(turns to Tanya)* and said, "Excuse me, I know this is forward of me, but I just want to tell you how beautiful you look today." *(turns to audience)* And then she starts getting all loud...

Tanya: How dare you approach me with such politeness and compliment me like that. *(turns to audience)* Stop. Rewind. It didn't even happen that way. What actually happened was—at least in my situation, God knows how many times he's done this before, but with me—I was just walking down the hall on my way to class minding my own business *(slowly walks toward Dan)*, when some *thing* blocked my path.

Dan: *(blocks Tanya's path)* Damn, where are you going?

Tanya: To class.

Dan: No, you're not. I think you're staying here, talking to me. Damn, baby—you look good. But you know that.

Tanya: *(annoyed)* Yeah. Thanks. *(tries to go around Dan)*

Dan: Real good. *(Dan grabs Tanya's butt. She walks back, revealing his outstretched hand frozen at butt level.)*

Dan: *(looks guiltily at the audience)* What ??!!

Tanya: *(turns to audience)* Once you touch me, you cross the line past a simple compliment. And I told him *(turns to Dan)*: Don't you ever put your hands on me.

Dan: All I did was give her a friendly tap, showing my appreciation for her good looks.

Tanya: Well, if your "love tap" touches any part of my body, you've gone too far. *(turns to audience)* And once you touch me against my wishes, you disrespect me. *(turns to Dan)* Unfortunately for you, I'm not one to keep my mouth shut.

Dan: *(turns to audience, upset)* She reported me to the dean. This whole thing has been blown out of proportion. I just want to ask you how one little situation turned into this whole big argument. Why are you making this such a big deal?

Tanya: Respect *is* a big deal. You should've given me the same respect you would give your little sister or your mother. You know what, one day your thirteen-year-old daughter is going to come home and tell you a guy she didn't even know came out of nowhere and tried to feel her up in the hallway at school. How are you gonna feel then?

Making the

Judy: There is a boundary line. If a guy says "Hi," it's cool. But once this guy came up to me and said, "I'm gonna touch your tits." That is simply disrespectful. If someone talks to you, it's annoying but okay. But when you feel that you have to cover yourself, it's gone too far.

Alex: It drives me crazy when I pass a woman in the street at night and it's so clear she's afraid. I mean, I'd like to walk her home to make sure nothing happens to her! And yet, there's no way to bridge that fear.

Canedy: I'm terrified when guys talk to me on the street at night.

Hassan: I was on the train and the girls came up to me and started kicking it to me like I was the girl and they were the guys. I felt really offended—they expected that simply because they were females, I was going to be appreciative of the attention and naturally want to hang with them. They didn't expect me to have any taste or opinion of my own about the situation.

Darniece: My brother came home furious the other day because some girls he was looking at pinched his butt as he was getting off the bus. Now, my brother does that to girls all the time. And you wouldn't believe how angry he was simply because the roles were reversed.

Donald: I'm sorry, I think your brother got what he deserved. What goes around comes around.

Jamaul: Nobody deserves to be violated. You would never say that about a female.

First Move

Do you like to make the first move?

CITY KIDS SURVEY SAYS:

Yes	No	Sometimes
ℍℍ ℍℍ ǁ	ℍℍ ℍℍ ℍℍ	ℍℍ ǀ

What makes someone attractive to you?

CITY KIDS SURVEY SAYS:

eyes — BIG BUTT! — maturity
tallness
Nice Smile
great legs
cool hair
lips — their style & attitude
sense of humor — the INSIDE counts

QUICK TAKES

How do you ask someone out?

- Go up to them and ask.
- Get your friend to do the dirty work.
- Call them up.
- Casually invite them over to your house to do homework.
- Write them a note.

QUICK TAKES

The way to get someone to notice you is to . . .

- drop something in front of them.
- make them laugh.
- hang out with their friends.
- bump into them "by accident."
- tease them.
- write them a corny love letter.
- give them flowers.
- feed them a line.
- make up an excuse to call them on the phone.
- dedicate a song to them on the radio.

THE CHASE

▶ ▶ ▶ ▶

QUICK TAKES

Do you live for the chase?

- Well, if you can get a girl easily, then she is not worthy of you.
- If I've gone out of my way for a guy, I'll keep him. Usually.
- I don't chase guys, but once I get them, then I turn them down. I always do it.
- I'm a bad, bad boy. But once I thought I was bored with this girl, but then I really did like her. I didn't get her back.
- I get a few girls at a time. I always talk to a lot of girls.
- Fooling around ain't about liking your partner any more. It's about kicking it to a girl and getting away with it. It's a skill you develop. When you get better at it, you're a man.
- It depends on how I feel.
- I don't get bored with girls. I want them. I hate that I want them.
- I don't play that game. I want someone because I want to be with them.

> The people who love only once in their lives are really the shallow people. What they call their loyalty and fidelity, I call either the lethargy of custom or their lack of imagination.
>
> —Oscar Wilde

! ! ! ! True Stories ! ! ! !

I went out with this one guy who treated me wonderfully in the beginning: he wrote me love letters, called all the time, and surprised me with little presents. But as time went by, he totally changed. He became this jerk who always was busy when I called and who said bad things about me to his friends. By that time I was so in love (or so I thought), that I couldn't break up with him. I really woke up when he took another girl to his senior prom. That hurt gave me the confidence to tell him exactly what I thought about him. At first I missed him, but life really does go on.

Melynda, 17

QUICK  TAKES

People date jerks because . . .

- of the status (those are the cool guys).
- girls like the challenge.
- where there's anger, there's passion.
- they like the hunt.
- it's the only way they know how to get attention.
- jerks can't be caught—it sparks your ego and sense of conquest.
- it's a control thing.
- they think you can tame them.
- they're addicted to wild natures.

QUICK  TAKES

How does it feel to want someone you can't have?

- It's so frustrating you could die.
- Something about the chase—you want it so badly, then when you get it you con't want it anymore.
- You want to send messages to the brain.
- You want to grab them and say, "I'm here! I'd be great for you!" But you can't—especially if you go to the same school.
- It can be a learning experience.
- Sometimes you feel it's all for nothing.

The Perfect Date

! ! ! ! ! True Stories ! ! ! !

I've been on a lot of dates in my life: I've spent the whole night in a diner and had a great time. I've gone to a fancy place and spent a lot of money and had a terrible time. I've had a woman pay for everything and not wanted to see her again. I just want to be able to relate to the person I'm with and not feel any barriers. I just don't want to have to worry about anything, not have to have too much small talk.

Mikel, 19

My favorite dates are when I go to my boyfriend's house on Sunday at 11:30 or noon. We eat breakfast and spend the rest of the day watching football, having little "arguments," and teasing each other when our teams are losing. Later, we eat dinner, watch the 8 pm game, cuddle, and then I go home.

Aleccia, 16

SPEAK YOUR MIND

What's your idea of the perfect date?

My dream date…a weekend at a resort. Combining nature, elegance, and seclusion.

Julia, 16

Dinner's always good. There's this little homey Italian spot round my way. Candlelight and talking. I like walks by the river a lot. Just sitting on a park bench. It'd be nice to go to some fancy place, but when you go somewhere they know you, that's the best.

Dash, 19

My boyfriend would pick me up from my house in a limo. He would have a dozen roses, one of each color, and a big box with a gorgeous outfit inside. We'd have dinner, go for a horse-and-buggy ride in the park, and go see a Broadway show. Then we'd go to a jazz club and dance all night.

Melynda,17

The most romantic date for me would be to take my girlfriend out, anywhere, and we'd see a lot of people that I know, and they'd see us, and I'd get to say to them, "Hi, this is my girlfriend."

Matthew, 18

He would pick me up and we'd go for a picnic on the beach. Talk, go dancing, hang out with friends. Then we'd go home and he'd kiss me goodnight.

Nicole, 16

what is LoVe?

Love Is ...

- finding someone who understands you.
- being with someone just like you—but better.
- when you care about someone else as much as you care about yourself.
- feeling like you've come home.
- right after "really like."
- an emotion that makes you do strange things.
- giving someone back the same happiness they give you.
- it's different for everyone.
- leaving yourself open.
- when two people dive into each other.
- a necessity to humanity.
- when you like somebody for personality, looks, and annoying habits.
- an emotional adventure.

What do you think of when you hear the word "LOVE"?

CITYKIDS SURVEY SAYS:

Makes you cry
Yeah, right!
Feels good!
Unconditional
never had it...
happy
Never will be
beautiful

She loves...
me not...

SPEAK YOUR MIND

People say you just feel it, feel this passion inside you. I haven't been out with that many people, and I haven't felt that spasm of love.

Mario, 16

I think love is overrated. People are always hunting for love. It's at the point where you're not looking for it, when you don't expect it, that it comes. I think that people should learn something from that. It doesn't have to be the white-picket-fence thing, either—love comes up in different ways.

Philippe, 18

Love is not only a feeling, it takes you over. It becomes the blood in your veins. Every hidden place in your body tingles. When love takes you over, you become numb, like your body is reconstructing its whole system to deal with this feeling. Everything shuts off. Then after the reconstructing is over, your body is built for love. Love takes up every waking moment. Every unconscious moment. That is the meaning of love to me.

Laura, 17

She loves me...

She loves me not...

She loves me...

She loves me not...

Love does not consist in gazing at each other but in looking together in the same direction.
—Antoine de Saint-Exupéry

Love is mutually feeding each other, not one living on another like a ghoul.
—Bessie Head

HOW Do You Know

When I'm in love with someone, he's almost all I think about, I want to see him or at least talk to him all of the time. I don't fall in love often, but when I do, I fall hard.

Natalie, 15

You know when you're in love when they're always with you. They get on your nerves, and you want them to leave, so then they leave and 30 seconds later you miss them. When you think of them, you get a tingly feeling in your stomach and it's not a constipation feeling, it's not a stomach pain. You find yourself doing things that you absolutely hate but it's for the other person. You find yourself compromising major beliefs and not necessarily caring and you're blinded and tend to ignore family and friends.

Christopher, 17

Well, to me it's when my girl (or lady) and I reach that level where all of our feelings are made as one, then I feel different about both myself and my girl. Certain ways tend to change and everything is somehow directed or involving her and vice versa. She would be everything to me, my joy and my pain. Meaning that I'll love her through the joyous times, most definitely, and the painful ones. However, the love would no doubt still be there. That will never change unless we're breaking up. Now that's another story!

Daniel, 17

When You're in Love?

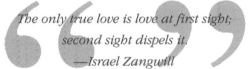

I know I'm in love when...

- I'm deep—it can be after a day, a year, a week.
- I look no further.
- I'm thinking about the person when I should be doing something else.
- I'm with someone and no one else matters.
- I want to see her all the time, I want to call her, and I'm worried about bugging her.
- she's the bright spot, no matter how difficult life is.
- it doesn't matter if I hate their clothes.
- I'm willing to sit through a Billy Ray Cyrus concert.

Do you believe in love at first sight?

CITY KIDS SURVEY SAYS:

Yes	No	Maybe
ΗΗ		
ΗΗ	ΗΗ	ΗΗ
	ΗΗ	
ΗΗ	ΗΗ	I
ΗΗ	III	

Love Quotes

It has been wisely said that we cannot really love anybody at whom we never laugh.—Agnes Repplier

We love because it is the only true adventure. —Rainer Maria Rilke

Love: a grave mental disease.—Plato

Kwenda ti kwendithio (Love cannot be forced). —Gikuyu proverb

Love without esteem cannot go far or reach high. It is an angel with only one wing.—Alexandre Dumas, *fils*

Love is an irresistible desire to be irresistibly desired. —Robert Frost

There are all kinds of love in this world, but never the same love twice.—F. Scott Fitzgerald

We can only learn to love by loving.—Doris Murdock

Men learn to love the women they are attracted to and women become attracted to the men they love.—*sex, lies and videotape*

The greatest love is a mother's, then comes a dog's, then comes a sweetheart's.—Polish proverb

Women and men...men and women. It will never work.—Erica Jong

First love is only a little foolishness and a lot of curiosity.—George Bernard Shaw

Love is as strict as acting. If you want to love somebody, stand there and do it. If you don't, don't. There are no other choices.—Tyne Daly

It is not love, but lack of love, which is blind.—Glenway Wescott

I wish I'd a knowed more people. I would of loved 'em all.
If I'd a knowed more, I woulda loved more. —Toni Morrison

To love is to stop comparing.—Merrit Malloy

First love is a kind of vaccination that immunizes a man from catching the
disease a second time.—Honoré de Balzac

Love is like an hourglass, with the heart filling up as the brain empties.—Jules Renard

What's love got to do with it?
—Song lyric, sung by Tina Turner

There is no greater experience than to be wanted.
—Moondog, New York City street poet

Love has the power of making you believe what you would
normally treat with the deepest suspicion. —Count de Mirabeau

As to marriage or celibacy, let a man take which course
he will, he will be sure to repent.—Socrates

Hate is not the opposite of love, apathy is.
—Rollo May

A girl can wait for the right man to come along, but in the meantime that still
doesn't mean she can't have a wonderful time with all the wrong ones.—Cher

Love is the state in which man sees things most decidedly
as they are not.—F. W. Nietzsche

Love and work...work and love, that's all there is.—Sigmund Freud

It's a good thing that love is blind, otherwise it would see too much.—Anon.

Can you imagine a world without men? No crime
and lots of happy fat women.—Marion Smith

Where
did
YOU
learn
about
SEX?

QUICK TAKES

I learned about sex from . . .

- a fool named Justin who exaggerated a lot.
- my sister.
- well, I learned all the *correct* things about sex from the AIDS education group I belong to.
- girls I messed around with.
- I don't remember. My boyfriend in kinder-garten showed me his penis on the school bus. I've always been sexual.
- everywhere.
- a book about fetus development. I didn't believe it. I had to go to another book to check.

QUICK TAKES

Do you think people shouldn't have sex before a certain age?

- No, but I do think you have to reach a certain maturity. Different people reach it at different ages. I don't think I have yet.
- You shouldn't have sex until you feel you're emotionally ready to handle it, but at the same time, I don't think you're always mature enough to make the best decision.
- Yes, like, your mind can't handle sex when you're eleven.

QUICK
TAKES

Did your parents give you "the talk"?

- Sort of, they told me that I should be careful and trust my instincts.
- I never felt comfortable talking to my parents about it, so I never started a conversation. I guess they never felt comfortable either.
- My mother did. I remember laughing because she brought it up when we were watching TV, or something. She really was reassuring me that I could tell her or ask her anything.
- Not from Mom at all, but Dad tried. All I remember is that he tried.
- My mom told me that sex is good, but girls would try to trap me, and AIDS ain't good.
- Kinda, I blocked it out.
- My parents gave me the book *Where Do Babies Come From?* In it, the eggs wore bridal gowns and the sperm wore tuxedos, and only one sperm got the egg.
- My mom just told me about getting my period, but she certainly did not tell what could happen or where babies come from.
- I sort of figured it out myself when I was eight years old.
- When I was ten my mom had me read a pink-and-blue book that had pictures to illustrate the diversity of intercourse. Then my mom wanted to discuss it. It was very embarrassing.

some little white

Friendship and sex don't go together.

Only freaks masturbate.

You can get pregnant from a toilet seat.

Girls who wear tight clothing are asking for it.

Talking about sex spoils the fun.

Sex lasts as long as it does in the movies.

You can't kiss people with braces.

Sex and love are the same thing.

All girls are teases.

Virgins know nothing about sex.

Babies come from the hospital.

Birds and bees have sex together.

LIES!

All girls are submissive.

Sex is the most important thing in a relationship.

"No" always means "yes."

Kissing will get you pregnant.

People choose to be gay.

Guys have urges they just can't control.

You can't get pregnant the first time.

If you have sex before you are married, no one will marry you.

All girls play mind games.

The stork brought me.

All guys want is sex.

Whab' The Big

Why are females so scared of sex?

- They are?
- We are?
- Maybe we're just hesitant. We have reason to be.
- Because all guys seem to think about is sex!
- Pregnancy, diseases, giving themselves away.
- I know plenty of situations in which the girl is really gung-ho about having sex.
- I'm just afraid physically.
- 'Cause boys have been taught that it's a masculine thing to do and girls are told that it's a slut thing to do.
- It all boils down to anatomy.
- Girls aren't afraid of sex, just guys' attitude about sex.
- Most women have been violated in some way at some point, so sex is scary.
- It's a lot easier for women to get diseases (not to mention getting pregnant).
- Men just have more authority in their minds, so it seems as though they can't get hurt.

> *People don't need sex as much as they need to be listened to.*
> *—Jane Wagner*

Deal About Sex?

QUICK TAKES

Why do males want to have sex so much?

- It's an ego thing.
- They just love the idea of it, it makes them feel good.
- Some of them are curious.
- I know a lot of times when the guy is all talk, and when it comes down to it, he's scared.
- Their sexual peak is at seventeen or eighteen, their hormones are raging.
- Females want sex a lot, too.
- It's hard to say "males" as one big category, since many males are scared to have sex also; there are reasons to be, what with diseases and all.
- Umm…they enjoy it, maybe?
- It's a way for them to feel loved.

When I found out that a friend of mine had AIDS, all I felt at first was shock.

I was really ignorant about AIDS. I thought that only gay men could get

AIDS. Then I was mad at her because I knew she didn't take precautions.

I felt scared because I know she's going to die. I couldn't speak to her.

I blamed her and avoided her. After a while, I learned about AIDS, and I

talked to some of my other friends about her. Then I thought, "She's going

to die and I should be there for her." The sad part is that she hadn't slept

with many guys. The time she got AIDS she slept with this guy once, and

from that her life was over. The more I see her, the more respect I have for

her. If it was me, I don't really know if I could go on. It's hard to fight day

after day, knowing that you're going to die. Now I just try to be helpful and

supportive, and above all, I try to be a true friend.

Safe sex is romantic 'cause dying is unromantic.

—Cenophia, 17

—Laura, 17

REALITY

● ● ● ●

I want to recognize a woman's right not *to share or express her sexuality and be able to do so without fear of reproach...It* **"** *can be a place of healing, of intense spiritual growth, of caring and loving oneself sexually—whatever we need and want this space to be, it can be.* **"**
—Sabrina Sojourner

Interview with Sheela, 16, and Wes, 19

interview

Can you have a good relationship without sex?
Sheela: You don't have to do it to be happy with someone.

Wes: It can make some people feel closer. It's not necessary, but if it does happen, it's a real part of the relationship. It doesn't have to be going all the way, either. We can just be lying down watching TV together and show each other how we feel.

Sheela: It can ruin a relationship. People assume that becuase I'm sixteen, I'll be influenced by the age difference and throw myself at him.

Wes: People talked about us, saying stuff like, He's not gonna stay with her. She's a virgin.

Sheela: We broke a lot of stereotypes. Wes just said something really nice—it's not what you do, it's what's in your mind when you're touching each other.

Wes: She's my best friend.

Sheela: He's my best friend. Not caring about what everyone else thinks has made us so close.

Wes: If it were after a week or after a year, it would only matter if we were ready.

I know some people are sad about the first time. It wasn't like that for us. I love him and I wanted to share that experience with him. I also believe that if we didn't do it, we'd still be together.

Jenny, 19

Girls always complain that I'm going too slow. I waited months with my last girlfriend. It's happened to me twice that I've started something and the girl just didn't want to. I really don't want that to ever happen again—it makes me feel so bad. But I could just kiss a girl for six hours. I don't want to dog anyone. You gotta go back to the nice-guy book.

Dash, 19,

I've never had sex. It's not like I'm waiting until I get married or anything. I've just never had the chance to have sex. I had my first "real" relationship this summer while I was away. My boyfriend and I were going to have sex, but when he snuck out of his dorm on his way to mine, he got caught and sent back to his dorm. So it never happened, and I'm kind of glad that we didn't do it.

Sam, 16

SPEAK YOUR MIND

Sex…people think I'm crazy because I want to be a virgin until my wedding night—I'm starting to agree with them. Not to be so frank…but I'm one of the horniest toads on the face of this planet! There are times I want to ignore all the religious boundaries I've set for myself. Then there are other times when I want to find someone who looks half-decent to make love to, and ask God for forgiveness later. But I've held back so far, so I suppose I can hold out for another few years. Yield not to temptation….

Jenine, 17

If I trusted and loved him, and he was my best friend, I *might* consent to sex. But I would never have sex in a social situation, like a party or something.

Nicole, 14

BREAKING UP

I'm mad because I let myself get hurt. She didn't hurt me. I let myself be hurt. I really did want to make breaking up easier. So I tried to be nice and cool. But it wasn't until we were able to blow up at each other that we were able to get to a point where we had an understanding.

I learned something about relationships, though. That you have to define yourself first and *then* find someone to be with. Don't lie to yourself. Don't settle for anything less than what you want—even if it's harsh for the other person.

MATT, 19

MELYNDA, 17

From the beginning, it seemed like we'd be together for a long time. People change, though. I changed the way I felt. He changed the way he appeared. I still remember what it's like to love him. It makes me sad, but I've never regretted breaking up with him. I'm trying not to forget how good it was to be with him, but I don't want to be with him again. Trying to co-exist in the same place is really awkward now.

Now I know not to lose myself in a relationship. I was living for Matt. I was always try-ing to think of what I could do to make sure he didn't break up with me. I felt like I didn't live up to his expectations. He was look-ing for this ideal perfect woman. I tried to be that for a while. I put myself aside and he did, too. That's why we eventually broke up. We had nothing left.

GROWING

Interview with Liza, 17, and John, 21

What did you guys do on your first date?

Liza: He called me and asked me to go out after we'd been talking for around eight hours. We didn't want to go to the movies because everyone does that.

John: We went diner-hopping and got hot chocolate. And just walked around all over the place in the cold.

Liza: And then we went to the movies.

John: We went to see *Forever Young.* I think this is romantic. In the movie, Mel Gibson gives up the opportunity to ask this woman he loves to marry him. He stalls and stalls, and then the woman runs into the street and gets hit by a car.

Liza: That's when he decides to lean over and kiss me.

Why is this relationship different from others you've had?

Liza: It's lasted more than two months.

John: I wasn't the best person to girls before. I've changed a lot. I was never a bad person, but I'd kiss a girl, never call, never care.

Liza: I had just turned seventeen when we started going out and he was already twenty.

John: Stereotypically, girls who are seventeen don't know what they want. I know a lot of girls her age who go out every Friday and Saturday night looking for guys. Liza's not like that.

What's difficult about being in a relationship?

John: Sometimes I think too much about losing each other. I get insecure.

Liza: We're constantly worrying if we're making each other happy.

John: Nothing's unbearable.

Liza: Everybody gets insecure. I recognize that I'm a good person and he's a good person. That gives me security.

How do you picture your future?

Liza: When I think of the future, I think of *my* future. I try not to picture John either way.

TOGETHER

I want a degree, that I know.

John: I think about our future a lot. If we'll be together. If I go on the road for a long time (I'm a musician), if that will affect us.

Liza: We plan for the immediate future.

John: We only joke about marriage.

Liza: Once you were serious.

John: If we were older. If we were financially secure.

What's the first thing you feel when you think about each other?

Liza: If I hear his music, I get excited. It's such a long ride to his house on the train. When I get near his house, I get a feeling of excitement in my stomach.

John (blushes): I don't know. If we don't see each other for a long time, I get that feeling. Butterflies or whatever. It's hard to explain. I love her so much. It's not a line. I know some things I say she says it's just a line. It's just good and I know it.

Last words?

John: If somebody reads this, they're going to think everything is hunky-dory. It is, for the most part. But people should know what to expect. We have our little spats, mostly over the stupidest things. That's the number one thing, though—communication.

Liza: There are big fights. Almost-breaking-up fights.

John: There are only two fights I can recall that were deep.

Liza: I recall three.

John: I joke too much about the wrong thing—that annoys you.

Liza: He's an actor, and when he jokes with me, it sounds serious. I get mad and start acting snotty, so he does the same.

John: Sometimes problems outside the relationship will make me quiet and make her think I don't care about her. When things get like that, I try to reassure her. I once took out some bad things on her. People say you take things out on the person you love most.

Liza: It's not just communication. It goes further than that. You have to do something about things that affect the other person.

John: Sometimes you forget, though.

HOW TO BECOME A CITYKID

If you live in or around New York City, you can walk right into the headquarters of the CityKids Foundation and become part of a group of young people who are moving on the world to make it a better place. If you want to join a CityKids Coalition meeting, come to 57 Leonard Street in Lower Manhattan any Friday between 4:30 and 6:30 P.M. and jump right into discussions and activities. You can also learn about how to host workshops with the CityKids Speak Team. And if you're into acting, singing, or dancing, you might even want to audition for the CityKids Repertory. In Repertory, you'll get the chance to perform the original music and dramatic material that carry CityKids' positive message to youth everywhere.

If you're not in the New York area, you can still become a part of CityKids by mail. You'll receive a quarterly update of CityKids news, appearances, community project ideas, conflict resolution tips, and more. For information on CityKids, send a stamped, self-addressed envelope to:

The CityKids Foundation
57 Leonard Street, New York, N.Y. 10013.

Most important, no matter where you live, being a CityKid is a state of mind. We believe in the power and potential of youth, social responsibility, breaking through racial barriers, friendship, humanity, positive influence, and the good in every individual. Come join us—and find out what you can do for CityKids and what CityKids can do for you!

CITYKIDS PUBLISHING COMMITTEE

Director: Laura Romanoff

Matt Alicardi
Angelica Benton-Molina
Alicia Brown
Charlene Fergus
Danielle Hayes
Dawn Hayes
Laura Johnson
Candy Knowles
Melynda Milman
Cenophia Mitchell
Jamaul Roots
Yadira Ruiz
Nachayka Vanterpool
Mikel Washington